The Bagel King

Inspired by the bagel fairy. He was the real thing. — A.L.

For Ziggy — S.N.

The Yiddish words in this book are:

mensch (*mentsh*): a good person

oy: expression or exclamation usually used in dismay

schmutz (*shmuhtz*): dirt or grime, usually spilled or dropped

tuches (*took-huss*): your bum

zaida (*zay-dah*): grandfather

Other things to know:

bagel (*bay-gull*): a ring-shaped bread roll traditionally made by boiling and then baking

chicken soup: a traditional Jewish home remedy for colds and anything else that might ail you. Usually served with noodles or fluffy round dumplings called matzo (*maht-zah*) balls.

Text © 2018 Andrew Larsen
Illustrations © 2018 Sandy Nichols

Kids Can Press gratefully acknowledges the financial support of the Government of Ontario, through the Ontario Media Development Corporation; the Ontario Arts Council; the Canada Council for the Arts; and the Government of Canada, through the CBF, for our publishing activity.

Published in Canada and the U.S. by Kids Can Press Ltd.
25 Dockside Drive, Toronto, ON M5A 0B5

Kids Can Press is a Corus Entertainment Inc. company

www.kidscanpress.com

The artwork in this book was rendered in acrylic paint. The text is set in Calisto.

Edited by Yvette Ghione
Designed by Julia Naimska

Printed and bound in Malaysia in 10/2017 by Tien Wah Press (Pte.) Ltd.

CM 18 0 9 8 7 6 5 4 3 2 1

FSC
www.fsc.org
MIX
Paper from responsible sources
FSC® C012700

Library and Archives Canada Cataloguing in Publication

Larsen, Andrew, 1960–, author
     The bagel king / written by Andrew Larsen ; illustrated by Sandy Nichols.

ISBN 978-1-77138-574-9 (hardcover)

     I. Nichols, Sandy, 1965–, illustrator II. Title.

PS8623.A77B34 2018   jC813'.6   C2017-903188-0

The Bagel King

Written by Andrew Larsen

Illustrated by Sandy Nichols

KIDS CAN PRESS

Every Sunday morning Zaida went to Merv's Bakery for bagels.

Sometimes Eli went with him.

Mrs. Rose would let Eli have a pickle from one of the big jars on the shelf behind the counter. Zaida said they were the best pickles in the world. Eli agreed.

Usually, though, Eli stayed home, and Zaida delivered the bagels right to his door.

Zaida brought bagels in winter, spring,
summer and fall.

He brought them through snow, rain, heat and gloom. Zaida had been bringing bagels for as long as Eli could remember.

Eli would hear a familiar *Knock! Knock!*
"Who's there?"
"It's me!" Zaida would say. "I've got bagels!"

Warm.
Chewy.
Salty.
Bagels were the best thing about Sunday.

One sunny Sunday morning Eli waited for that
familiar *Knock! Knock!* But it didn't come.

Eli grew hungrier with each passing minute.

He looked out the window, searching for Zaida.
But he didn't see him.

Instead, he saw Mrs. Katz.

She was digging a hole in her garden.

The phone rang. Eli ran to answer it. It was Zaida!
He had slipped on some schmutz at Merv's.
Mrs. Rose had seen it all happen from behind the
counter. She called the doctor.

The doctor said Zaida hurt his tuches and
had to rest at home for two whole weeks.

Eli rushed over to Zaida's.

"Are you okay?!" he asked, out of breath.

"Of course I'm okay," said Zaida. "But I didn't get the bagels."

Eli groaned. Zaida moaned. Their bellies grumbled and growled.

Knock! Knock!
"Who's there?"
It was Zaida's neighbors: Mr. Rubin, Mr. Wolf and Mr. Goldstick. They shuffled past Eli and into the living room, where Zaida was sitting on the sofa.

"I'm hungry," said Mr. Rubin.
"I'm famished," said Mr. Wolf.
"Let's eat!" said Mr. Goldstick.
"What's going on?" asked Eli.

"Every Sunday morning your zaida gets me a sesame seed bagel with smoked salmon," explained Mr. Rubin.

"He gets *me* a plain bagel with cream cheese," said Mr. Wolf.

"And a poppy seed bagel with pickled herring for me," said Mr. Goldstick. "Every Sunday morning we come to your zaida's apartment for a feast. We've been doing it for years."

"Well, there's no feasting today," Zaida told them.
"I fell on my tuches."

"Oy!" they exclaimed. "Are you all right?"

"Of course I'm all right," said Zaida. "But what's
a Sunday without bagels?"

"It's just another day," Eli said with a sigh.

Zaida followed the doctor's orders and rested. One day Eli brought chicken soup.

Another day Eli brought chicken soup and a book from the library.

Then later that week Eli brought more chicken
soup and a friend.

"What's with all the chicken soup?" asked Zaida.

"Chicken soup makes everything better," said Eli.

Zaida laughed as he rubbed his tuches.

"It makes most things better," he said.

On Saturday night Eli had bagels
on the brain.
    Even the moon looked like a bagel
all smothered with cream cheese.

On Sunday morning Eli woke up
extra early and made a list.

Zaida: poppy seed bagel with
cream cheese

Mr. Ruby: sesame seed bagel with
smoked salmon

Mr. Wolf: plain bagel with
cream cheese

Mr. Goldstick: poppy seed bagel
with pickled herring

Me: same as Zaida

Then he added one more thing.
It was going to be the perfect surprise.

Merv's Bakery was buzzing with business.
Eli saw a few familiar faces from the
neighborhood.

"Good morning, Eli," said Mrs. Rose. "Would you like a pickle? And how's your zaida?"

"He's fine," said Eli. "He's resting. I'm here to get some bagels. Can you help me?" Eli gave Mrs. Rose the list.

"This list looks very familiar," she said. "Except for the last item."

"It's a surprise for Zaida and his friends," said Eli.

"They'll love it!" said Mrs. Rose, with a twinkle in her eye.

Mrs. Rose prepared the order with care. She packed everything into a big brown paper bag and handed it to Eli.

"Watch your step," she said. "And say hello to your zaida for me."

"I will," said Eli. "Thanks, Mrs. Rose."

Eli cradled the bagels all the way to Zaida's.

Knock! Knock!
"Who's there?"
"It's me!" said Eli.
"Me who?"
"Me, Eli. I've got bagels!"

"Bagels?" gasped Zaida, opening the door.
"Bagels!" said Mr. Rubin, delighted.
"Come in, come in," said Mr. Wolf.

"What a mensch!" said
Mr. Goldstick. "The boy's a prince."

"I went to Merv's and got your
usual Sunday order," said Eli.

"The boy's no prince — he's
a king," Zaida proudly declared.
"He's the Bagel King!"

"Long live the Bagel King!"
they cheered.

"And I have a little surprise," added Eli,
reaching into the big brown paper bag.
"I brought a jar of Merv's pickles."

"All hail the mighty pickle!" Zaida
proclaimed.

Warm.
Chewy.
Salty.
Bagels were the best thing about Sunday.
The best thing, that is, except for Zaida.